TARZAN *the* MIGHTY

with **FRANK MERRILL** *and* **NATALIE KINGSTON**

AN ORIGINAL SERIAL PRODUCED BY UNIVERSAL PICTURES CORPN.
BY SPECIAL ARRANGEMENT WITH

EDGAR RICE BURROUGHS

AUTHOR OF "TARZAN OF THE APES" AND "THE CAVE GIRL"

Directed by JACK NELSON

Morgan

TARZAN THE MIGHTY

BY

ARTHUR B. REEVE

ERBVILLE PRESS
FIRST EDITION

"Tarzan the Mighty" is based on the film version of the 15 chapter serial, "Tarzan the Mighty". This is the COMPLETE newspaper serialization as it originally appeared.

TARZAN THE MIGHTY

CHAPTER I
JUNGLE KING

"**D**ANCE!"

The girl, a gleaming blonde beauty, figure full, delicate, voluptuously formed, clad in a single leopard skin, drew away from the menace of the eyes and voice of the dark white man, reversion to the elemental, a thousand miles from civilization.

"Dance, I tell you!" hissed Black John through his wolfish teeth.

Her eyes, deeper and more blue than any lake of the Dark Continent, shot a quick glance to the right. There lay the jungle, teeming with wild life, fascinating, mysterious with its keen, heartless struggle for existence crowned by the survival of the fittest. It was beautiful—and relentless.

Another quick glance to the left. There was

the stockade wrested by man from pitiless luxuriant nature. Mary Trevor saw the huts, the cabin to which she had been borne with her little brother Bobbie after the wreck of the liner "Empress," sole survivors picked up Black John, the beachcomber. In a great semi-circle before the thatched huts in the stockade squatted the black-skinned natives, on one side their Patriarch, on the other the drummers with their outlandish hollowed logs covered taut with goat skins.

They were waiting for Black John to call on the spirit gods of their ancestral jungle, waiting for him to demonstrate again the power of the white man's witchcraft.

"Dance!"

An instant her eyes turned heavenward as she wafted a prayer. Above swayed the tangle of tropical moss and rope-vines. It was a glorious wild picture of nature "where every prospect pleases—and only man is vile."

Black John seized Mary in viselike grip by the wrists.

"Dance! Dance at this ceremony of the Curse of Tarzan! The next time, remember, it will be the ceremony of our wedding. Dance—or I will call the priests and perform the ceremony—now!"

With his other hand he waved. The weird sound of the native drums accompanied by the clatter of spears and aboriginal musical instruments burst forth in a pandemonium of barbaric tempo.

Black John advanced into the center of the group, descendants of a pirate crew that had settled in the jungle generations ago, inter-married, now reduced to the primitive state of superstitious savages—a lost village. He himself, the wayward son of a noble British family, by his superior wit and shrewdness had made himself the leader of the tribe, pretending a mastery of witchcraft.

"Tarzan and his ape people are raiding our cattle!" he cried loudly. "They are destroying our fields. They must perish!" He hung on the word as if it alone would annihilate an enemy.

Still grasping Mary Trevor, the delicate, beautiful, high-strung American castaway, by the wrist, Black John continued to harangue and exhort the villagers.

He paused before a flat stone. Seizing a brand from the council fire he applied it suddenly to a little pile on the stone. Instantly there was a blinding flash and a column of smoke shot high up in the air. It was Black John's magic by way of casting a spell to set fire to some black gunpowder and overawe the villagers, as a prelude.

"This will cast a spell of terror against Tarzan," he shouted boldly. "A curse on Tarzan and his tribe! He will not dare to come near us now!"

The beating of the native drums rose in sharp staccato, the clashing of musical instruments and of spears, the weird music of native voices.

Black John pulled Mary forward by the wrist almost dislocating it by the savage force of his grasp. "Now," he whispered, "dance! Show them my power over the White Goddess who will win the favor of the Jungle Gods! Dance as you never danced before! Give it to them—all!"

Mary felt herself catapulted into the midst of the wild assemblage with the frenzied music. There was just time for one thought to flash through her mind in a split second. The dance of wild abandon was the least of many evils that might befall her. It would give her respite—if even for a day—and another day, what might another dawn bring forth?

Propelled by the force of Black John she caught herself, poised on one foot, balanced, whirled and was off in a dance that was a stone-age exaggeration of classical dancing posturings of old dance halls of Frisco, the tango, the maxixe of South America and wound up in the negro movements that had captured the white dancers as she threw into them the spirit of native Africa itself.

Enthralled, the natives watched and followed the white goddess.

Far off in the jungle whence the eyes of Mary Trevor could not penetrate nor the echo of the curse reverberate, in a crotch of a great tree perched the figure of a man. In his hands he held a grass rope. About his neck hung a wonderful hunting knife in a sheath suspended by a thong.

He looped the rope and let it fly out. It caught on the limb of another tree with a peculiar loop that fastened itself. He pulled it tight, swung in a quick arc to the ground, slacked the rope and with a deft twist pulled it off the limb and down.

Handsome and erect he stood, every muscle playing smoothly as he gathered his grass rope, coiled it, and slung it over his shoulder.

Suddenly above the multitudinous sounds of the jungle he heard something that set him in quick motion crashing through the tangle.

It was Teeka, the she-ape, belle of the jungle, giving a call for help. The man parted the fronds of underbrush in time to catch a glimpse of Taug, an interloper, strange to that part of the jungle, as the powerful arms of the ape grasped Teeka about to bear her off. Teeka chattered and screamed in terror.

An instant and the man with incredible quickness and strength was between them, facing Taug.

"Go back whence you came I, Tarzan, command!"

He stretched forth his arm with an imperious gesture. But it was the voice that would have arrested and held attention. It was a human voice—but these were no human words.

For of all the beasts he knew the language, knew their names and how to call them, knew their trials and all their dangers; helped them, played and lived and suffered.

This was Tarzan, the Mighty, King of the Jungle!

CHAPTER II
QUEEN OF HIS KIND

INTO the heart of the jungle, mysterious and fascinating, where Tantor, the elephant, prince of beasts, trumpeted to the herd, where Numa, the lion, ruler of his kind, preyed on man and beast, where lived the tiger, the rhinoceros, the crocodile, and above all the ape people who made up in shrewd cunning what they lacked in strength, years before had come two intrepid explorers, Lord and Lady Greystoke.

Delirious with the dread jungle fever, Lord Greystoke and Lady Rosalie tossed in their bunks in the cabin they had built. Scientists though they were and protected against the perils of the jungle, the science of their day had given them only imperfect protection from perils unseen, microscopic.

In a sudden silence, Rosalie staggered up from her bed, swayed across to her husband, so still, and took his hand. It was cold. She laid it down, tottered in a daze over to the bed where crooned little Edward, her baby born on the expedition. With a prayer on her lips she, too, collapsed on the floor, another martyr to the white man's conquest of the tropics.

Toka, the she-ape, had just been the victim of another jungle tragedy. Her own baby had fallen a victim to the dread foe of man and beast—death. Toka wandered, unconsoled, when suddenly from a strange habitation in her jungle she heard a piercing cry, a wail. It was not of an ape-child. Yet it was the young of some animal strangely akin. And it was the wail of hunger.

Toka looped over, looked in and entered. What she found stirred the depths of her already over-wrought mother heart. She picked up the baby, caressed it, fondled it, clasped it to her breast. There was none to say her nay. She loped off with her foundling man-child.

Through babyhood and childhood the foster-child of Toka grew. And, though he was the little friend of all the jungle world, yet the jungle knew he was different. Gradually as he grew to manhood in the life of the jungle, gleaning the rudiments of his own language from picture books left in the effects of his parents in the cabin, heir to the wonderful carved hunting knife of the dead sportsman, his father, gradually the jungle people came to realize that he was their king in brain and cunning, accepted the overlordship of Tarzan the Mighty, foster-child of Toka, the she-ape.

It was not often now that his power was questioned, except by Numa, who seemed to retain a hereditary enmity. That was why as Tarzan faced Taug, protecting Teeka, Tarzan laughed.

"Taug has chosen and there is none in the jungle to stay him!"

Quickly Tarzan's laughter changed to rage. Here was a defiance of his mandate to rule that he could not afford to pass.

Tarzan hit Taug a staggering blow. A moment and Taug was back at him. Again Tarzan hit him. Taug crumpled. In an instant Tarzan was over him, his Greystoke hunting knife unsheathed.

He felt his arm stayed. It was Teeka, pleading, for Taug. Slowly he returned the knife to its sheath, rose from the prostrate Taug and turned away. Again, as so often since he had reached the estate of manhood, swept over him the realization that neither the ape people nor the other beasts were his real kin.

Morose and moody Tarzan proceeded through the jungle. Now more than ever before he felt alone—all alone. These friends of the jungle were not his own people. Who were his own people?

Mechanically his course took him to the hut. Except for the ravages of time and the weather it was the same hut he remembered from earliest childhood. Something was vaguely stirring within him now as he entered. He picked up a child's picture book, glanced through it. It did not satisfy. On the table was a Bible, very worn and old. He opened it. There was a picture of a woman. He gazed at it long and earnestly. It stirred some recollections within him, indefinite, formless. Then, too, there was the picture of a man.

These were his people. For a long time he turned it over in his mind. Dead! Yes; without a doubt. But were there others?

He closed the book, put it back on the

table. Somehow now he was more alone than even he had been before. He felt he must get back into the jungle. At least there were his friends. Tantor, and the apes ...

Suddenly Tarzan paused. What was that strange new sound in the jungle? It was a voice—but the voice of no animal he knew and he knew them all.

There was something silvery, bell-like, about this voice. Nor was it mere repetition, like the calls of animals. It was always the same, yes—but it was always different. He stood a moment spellbound. He felt as if something were tugging at his heart. That voice! Why did it arouse such feelings within him? Other unfamiliar sounds aroused fear, wariness. But this, this seemed to fascinate, to lead him.

It came from close at hand, down the glen, down by the drinking pool. He took a step, then checked himself warily. Instead he swung himself upward by his grass rope into the tallest of the trees. From the top he could look over the edge, down into the pool.

Tarzan gripped the branch of the trees just in time to catch himself. Such a sight his eyes had never before looked upon. Never even in his wildest dreams had he had conceived anything so lovely, anything even remotely like it.

Standing stark, unclad, her little body poised just an instant on the edge of the pool that reflected back her gleaming white beauty stood Mary. Her dance completed she had fled from the stockade, thrown off her crude garment, prepared to plunge into the cooling waters as it were to wash from her the contamination of contact with Black John and his crew.

In the exuberance of her freedom she was trilling to herself some silvery ditty that recalled the civilization from which disaster had so rudely snatched her. It was this song of a human feminine voice that was new and sweet to the ear of Tarzan.

An instant and she slithered into the depths of the water of the pool striking out with a graceful crawl that left Tarzan speechless in admiration.

Suddenly his sharp eyes from his lofty perch caught a sight as from an airplane an observer might see a murderous submarine headed toward a graceful liner. Other eyes than Tarzan's had seen the girl. A huge crocodile was shooting straight from a dark eddy scenting a dainty morsel.

Tarzan uttered a cry, the cry with which he struck terror into the denizens of the jungle. Mary heard it, looked in time, saw the ferocious crocodile shooting with sea-plane speed at her, turned and headed for the shore.

At the same instant Tarzan leaped through the air in a high dive such as would have turned green with envy any stunt circus performer. Down—down—down he shot like a human projectile, plunged, turned upward, and grappled with the prince of the crocodiles just at the moment when those murderous jaws were within inches of snapping this queen of Tarzan's own kind, first he had ever seen in his marvellous winning of the jungle.

Over and over the man and the infuriated crocodile rolled in the water as Tarzan vainly struggled to grasp his knife from its sheath at some moment when the animal at home in his own element might be off guard. For Tarzan being off-guard for an instant might mean the loss of one of his own superbly developed limbs, perhaps of his life.

Mary, headed for safety and shore, looked back just in time to see a dozen or more of the crocodile tribe threshing after her so closely that it was scarcely an even break whether she could reach the shore first—and even then must she depend on a miraculous toughness of the slender tropical tangle of vines to pull herself well clear of those voracious, cruel jaws. She grasped the tangle and it parted in her hands as she screamed in frantic terror at the snapping jaws only a few inches behind her.

CHAPTER III
BLACK JOHN PLOTS

FRANTICALLY, desperately, Mary clutched at the tangle of vines again. This time it gave a little, but it held and she pulled herself safely up the bank just missing the ravening jaws of the foremost of the crocodiles by inches.

Still a-tremble like an aspen leaf in the wind she ran through the brush and with shaking fingers donned her scant garment of leopard skin, fastening it as she peered through the tangle at the handsome and heroic figure of a man as he struggled, waited his chance, then overcame the infuriated leader of the crocodiles, flung him back and with powerful strokes made the edge of the pool and drew his powerful form glistening with the water up to safety also.

He stood looking about for her, caught a glimpse of her as she drew back in the shadows. She started to run in sudden fear as he advanced toward her. He stopped, raised his hand and called.

"Fear not! Tarzan will not harm you!"

Mary hesitated. There was something at once commanding and reassuring in the tone. A smile, half-frightened, fitted over her face. She was tempted to wait, then her fears overwhelmed her. She waved her hand at him—and ran on toward the stockade.

Tarzan checked himself. A long time he gazed after her with a wondering, entranced expression on his face, then turned back again to his jungle—but not the same Tarzan he had been a scant half hour ago. A new purpose had come into his life.

Mary, too, at the entrance to the stockade paused to look back, with a smile at the memory of Tarzan. Perhaps she should have stayed. But then there was Bobbie. She turned.

Black John was glaring at her suspiciously.

"You've been outside the stockade again! Haven't I warned you enough of this Tarzan beast that's roaming around?"

Mary hid a sudden start at the uncanny mention of Tarzan. But she could not check the peculiar smile on her lips nor the shrug of her defiant shoulders even by her non-committal answer.

A gloating smile spread over the face of Black John. "This Tarzan ape is no match for Black John!" he boasted. "Even now I am waiting for word that he has been caught!"

Mary repressed a reply and hastened to the hut and to Bobby.

Deep in the jungle two of the cleverest of the natives had finished placing a trap cage and lay hidden in the brush watching it. They crouched entirely hidden as they heard the approach of something.

It was Taug making his way through, cautiously after his defeat by Tarzan in his attempt to gain the title of king of the jungle. Taug paused and stared curiously. Just before him he caught sight of a tempting bunch of jungle fruit, left unguarded by someone.

He moved forward for it, reached out to grasp it—and the door of the trap sprang shut as the ape lashed his way back and forth in futile effort now to free himself.

Instantly the two natives were on their feet. "Tarzan is caught!" cried one. "The Witch

Doctor is mightier than Tarzan the Mighty! Run and tell him while I guard the trap."

From a-far now Tarzan himself could hear the raging of Taug. Something was wrong—was it with this interloper or with some new claimant for the title of jungle king? Quickly Tarzan swung himself along in the direction of the cries.

Soon he was peering down from his eyrie in a tree whence he had swung himself by his grass rope. Below he could see the native in a dance of triumph about the cage-trap. A cunning expression over-spread Tarzan's features as he set himself for a long swing.

As though from the sky above Tarzan swung down upon the native guarding the trap. A look of frantic fear came to the native's face. It was as if by a miracle the supposed captive was free. In desperation he closed with Tarzan. But it was an unequal fight. A moment and Tarzan had picked him up bodily and flung him toward the cage.

The native lay there, still. Tarzan darted to the cage and peered in. It was Taug. "So," he muttered as he tore at the trap, "you would be king of the jungle!" Tarzan smiled. "Yet Tarzan is glad to help Taug."

Tarzan at last laid his hand on the catch of the trap. He unfastened the door, lifted it, and Taug sprang out.

It was no longer the sullen Taug. "Taug will fight Tarzan no more!" he chattered. "Tarzan is Tarzan the Mighty, mightier than Taug!"

Tarzan was an easy master. "Come!" he ordered. "When our enemies come they shall not find their trap empty!"

He picked up the unconscious native, carried him to the door of the trap, flung him in and closed it. He motioned to Taug to disappear, then Tarzan himself swung back by his grass rope up into the crotch of the tree and settled himself, unseen, to watch.

Into the stockade of the Lost Village dashed the breathless native runner calling at the top of his voice.

"Tarzan—Tarzan, the Mighty, is caught!"

Instantly the village was in an uproar. Within the hut Mary and Bobby heard. Mary drew Bobby close to her as they peered out at the excitement.

There was Black John surrounded by the admiring villagers. "Come on!" he harangued. "We will get this Tarzan who has been leading the beasts of the jungle against us! You shall see that I am mightier than this Tarzan the Mighty!"

"Tarzan!" whispered Bobby. "Why, Mary, that's the one saved you from the crocodile, isn't it?"

Heading the natives Black John was leading off the rabble.

"Yes, Bobbie. Let us go, too." Mary was worried.

They overtook the crowd just as Black John rushed up to the trap. Black John started to open it, posting the others ready to attack, capture and kill Tarzan. But it was only a moment before Black John's triumph changed to cries of baffled rage. No one came out. Black John reached in, dragging out now only the half conscious native.

"Why, it's one of the tribe!" exclaimed Bobby in surprise.

Mary was unable to restrain the relief she felt after her anxiety.

"It—it was Tarzan—with the strength of a million devils!" chattered the frightened native.

Black John hurled him away from himself and glared at the superstitious natives. He turned suddenly and an ugly scowl spread over his face as he caught the smile of Mary and Bobby's grin. Her smile changed quickly to alarm. Bobby shrank by her side.

"Laugh, will you?" Black John gripped Mary's wrists, glaring at her. "Mark this—no wild beast of the jungle can trick Black John!"

In terror Mary shrank away. Would the arch villain vent his rage on her and her little brother? What could she do? There was no one to whom to appeal—none.

None? A protector was closer than either she or Black John realized. High overhead hid Tarzan himself in the leafy screen of the trees. He saw; also he saw the tribe, too many for him.

But Tarzan, king of the jungle, was never defeated, not in his own jungle. His face was suddenly convulsed with rage at the indignity to the fair white queen. He raised his head and uttered a loud roar. It was human yet like nothing human. It was the battle cry of the king of the jungle calling upon his followers.

The natives heard and they knew it. They

fled in panic. Black John followed. Was he not their leader? In terror, too, Mary and Bobby fled.

Far and wide through his jungle kingdom the call was heard. Tantor heard and started, trumpeting.

Tarzan swung himself down before Mary and Bobby, stood before them in awed admiration. Mary did not know whether to run or stay. Bobby stared in wide-eyed fear and admiration.

"Fear not! Tarzan will never allow that Black John to harm the White Angel!"

Mary shivered at the thought of Black John. "You are good—good as you are brave. But Black John has many men—and you are alone."

Just then Tantor broke through the jungle. Tarzan smiled. "Tarzan is not alone! The beasts of the jungle are his friends! See!" Mary shrank back and Bobby cried out in fear. "Don't be afraid of Tantor. He is Tarzan's friend and will help the White Angel, even as Tarzan once helped him. Once when I was a very little boy, with my knife I cut him loose from a trap."

Quickly in his curious English Tarzan told the story. "And now," he added to Mary, "learn this bird call. If Tarzan hears the bird call, he will know the White Angel is in danger and will come."

Mary repeated the call until she got it perfect. But she was nervous. Her absence from the village would be noticed. She thanked Tarzan, turned toward the village, while Tarzan was swung up on his back by Tantor who started off, also.

In the thicket the jealous, scowling, scheming eyes of Black John missed none of this meeting. Through his tortuous brain was evolving a dark scheme. He would use Tantor to capture Tarzan and nip this friendship in the bud.

No sooner did Black John have an idea than he put it in execution. In the fastness of the Jungle he set the tribe to work digging a pit. In the bottom of the pit he placed rows of long, sharp-pointed stakes. Over the pit they laid a flimsy false floor of jungle foliage.

It was impossible to keep secret such a plot in the village. The moment Mary learned it her first thought was to warn Tarzan. She stole cautiously to the door of the hut and looked out. There on guard a burly native blocked her exit. She was a prisoner.

Somehow she must convey the warning to Tarzan. She looked helplessly at Bobby. Suddenly an idea flashed into her mind.

"They'll never suspect you, Bobby. Go—give the bird call. Tarzan will hear it and come to you. Warn him."

There was not much time to act. Already the natives had been posted through the jungle, first to scare up and worry Tantor, then to drive him down the trail that passed over the pit.

It would have taken a far more clever plotter than Black John to keep Tarzan entirely in the dark. Something was afoot in the jungle. That he knew. What it was, was for him to find out. Swinging along from the ground to the tree tops where he might catch sight of what was going on, Tarzan's practiced eyes were arrested by something unnatural in the old trail. He descended to investigate. Treading gingerly he started to lift the ground foliage. It was wilted. In an instant he saw why. Underneath was hidden a pit trap.

Could it have been prepared for him? Tarzan smiled as he swung himself back into the tree. He would stick around and watch what happened. There was an atmosphere of something portentous impending in the jungle. The beasts seemed to scent it. They were restless, uncertain. Far-off, somewhere, he could hear the faint echo of Tantor, trumpeting.

Suddenly he heard the bird call. He sought quickly to place it. It was near. His eyes endeavored to penetrate the jungle screen. There was Bobbie, running along the old trail— nearer and nearer the trap—the very trap of which he had come to warn Tarzan.

Tarzan shot out his coiled rope, caught another tree, pulled the rope taut, swung down on the end by one hand and with the free arm caught Bobbie, carried him on and up safe over the trap and landed on the limb of another tree over it.

There was not time for explanations. Tantor with a mob of the natives in full cry was now on the old trail, thundering down seeking escape and running closer and closer to capture and perhaps sudden death.

Tarzan shouted a warning. Tantor stopped, short, got it, turned and crashed through the jungle itself on another course.

Out on the limb Tarzan smiled to himself at the defeat of his enemies in the nick of time. The limb swayed and bent under him. At least he had caught the attention of Tantor just in time, and had save him.

There was a cracking and rending.

Tarzan had just time to seize Bobbie as the limb of the tree tore itself loose and the two were dropped down straight below into the very trap that had been set for Tantor.

CHAPTER IV
A PAWN OF PASSION

TARZAN landed, cat-like, on his feet in the bottom of the elephant pit, unscathed. Instantly he roused himself from the shock of falling and landing, shook himself like a wild-animal and looked about on guard.

He caught sight of Bobbie, lying unconscious where he had narrowly missed one of the murderous pointed stakes prepared for Tantor. Tarzan picked up Bobby in one arm and climbed out of the pit. He peered cautiously about, saw the natives had fled, then struck out into the jungle carrying the boy. A few moments later he staggered with his burden into the hut. Instinctively he began rubbing his head and hands to revive him.

In the village Black John full of anger and lust caught sight of Mary Trevor anxiously waiting for Bobby. "Say nothing to her of the boy, her brother," he growled to the natives, as he strode over toward her cabin.

"Where's Bobby?" faltered Mary backing away from him.

"Never mind about the boy, now. I have other things to talk of with you!" He leaned closer toward her and she backed away as far as the wall would permit from his repulsive self. "I have long wanted to make you my mate. Now I am going to claim you, before the tribe."

"No! No!" She was horrified, filled with loathing. "Not Yet!"

"Yes! Now! If you do not consent you will never see your brother again! I alone know where he is!"

Stunned, wide-eyed Mary stared as he turned abruptly and stamped out of the cabin. What should she do? She felt she could not hold out against him very long.

What a night it was! Bobby had not returned. Was he alive or dead? She could not get out of the cabin to give the bird call to summon Tarzan. She could not even search for Bobbie. And facing her was the nightmare of Black John and his imperious evil passion. Again and again she called upon heaven to return

Bobby to her. If she only had Bobbie she might flee with him into the jungle—anything was better than this living death.

"There's only one way to get your brother back!" Black John had heard her prayers and entered. Too broken and worn-out to resist she no longer could struggle when he put his arms about her. Black John took it as consent. "I will tell the Patriarch!" he decided gruffly. "We will hold the ceremony tonight!"

Mary made no sign. There was no hope now. Black John rose to go, leaving her crushed, with bowed head.

A few moments later he returned with the bearded Patriarch of the tribe and they began to arrange the wedding ceremonies in accordance with the tribal customs. Mary was dull and listless. Black John eyed her eagerly, covetously.

The day was worse than the night. She could not eat. She could not think. She could not even cry. She was too beaten it seemed, almost, to fight.

Listless, hopeless, Mary listened all day to the preparations for the terrible farce that marked the supreme tragedy for her.

Nightfall witnessed the village a-glare with fires and flares. The tribe had assembled in a huge circle about the spot where the Patriarch sat by the central fire, leaving a huge cleared circle. Beside him sat Black John, the crafty and cunning.

Resistance was useless as Mary was led on from the cabin, a burly black native on either side of her. In the firelight her beautiful white skin and delicately formed limbs gleamed against the blackness of the night. Black John's eyes gloated as he rubbed his grimy hands in anticipation of possessing anything as lovely as this girl clad in her scant leopard-skin. In silence the tribesmen watched as she was led past them.

"Dance!" thundered the Patri-arch.

"Dance!" prodded the two burly blacks.

Though she felt like fleeing into the night terror of the jungle and would have welcomed it if the earth had opened up and swallowed her, Mary started her dance. The tribe leaned forward in fascination. Black John bent his sinister eyes on her as she swept around before him, her master-to-be.

Mary met his gaze, quickly dropped her

eyes from his. She could not bear even to look upon the monster. Yet she dared not stop. What tortures or indignities might be in store for her from the fanatical followers of Black John, once he spoke the word?

Round and round she danced as she had been instructed by the Patriarch. Never was a dance with more leaden, unwilling feet. Yet Mary could not have been ungraceful no matter how she tried.

She knew the sharp eyes of both Black John and the Patriarch were upon her. There was nothing but pain and death to be accomplished by refusing the dance. Then what would become of Bobby?

She ended the dance by throwing herself on the ground at Black John's feet in the so-called ancient tribal manner as she had been instructed. It was the outward sign that she gave herself to him.

In crude, coarse triumph he looked at the lovely girl at his scrawny feet. Then he slowly rose until his bloated face and torso towered above her slight form.

"In accordance with our custom, this

woman has chosen me!" he bellowed. "And I claim her before you all!" Black John moved forward a step or two in the center of the circle. "And, also, in accordance with our custom I will meet any of you in fair combat for her!"

Black John paused in boastful defiance and looked around the circle. Mary, too, now for the first time raised her head. She also looked around as if hoping someone even a burly black or a lascar, might offer himself to do battle for her.

None made a move to get up.

Mary was disappointed; Black John triumphant. With a cheaply regal flourish he leaned down and raised her up. Every womanly instinct in her revolted. She felt a cold shiver convulse her body at his mere touch.

What a hollow mockery was all the mummery. Hollow? It was only too real, this nuptial mass of Devil.

Was she Black John's wife?

She felt herself swaying, going…

CHAPTER V
TANTOR TRUMPETS

BOBBIE regained consciousness in the hut of Tarzan. He looked frightened at first at the strange surroundings, then seeing it was Tarzan holding him was reassured.

The face of Tarzan was a study. It was a new sensation that he was experiencing, this contact with his own kind. There had dawned in him that instinct which responds to the call of humanity to protect the weak against the strong, the eternal conflict of good and evil. Tarzan was starting in with the fundamental passions, love and hate, hope and fear, courage and cowardice, virtue and vice, benevolence and malevolence.

"I want Mary," cried Bobbie, "take me to her." Again and again he tried to make Tarzan understand but could not.

Once he went to the door of the hut, struck out into the jungle but stopped suddenly as he caught a glimpse of Numa, the lion, snarling.

Tarzan heard it, too, leaped into action, grabbing Bobby in the nick of time, glaring at Numa who slunk away.

Bobby was willing enough now to return to the hut and together they spent the night, a strange pair, this man and boy.

In the morning when Bobby discovered the old picture book the roles were reversed. Here was the child instructing the man. As picture after picture was turned up Bobby found he had an apt pupil.

First it was a picture of a boy. There was no difficulty in getting the idea over with that. Next a girl. The next idea was therefore of Mary. Tarzan himself spied a picture of an ape. But Bobby shook his head, turned the pages, found a man. Quickly they agreed on the difference. These were all new ideas to Tarzan's keen mind. He absorbed them rapidly.

But still that was not what Bobby wanted to convey. Quickly he turned the pages. Ah, there was what he wanted, fortunately. It was a picture of a girl struggling with a man. With signs and gestures Bobby tried to get over what was in his mind.

"Mary needs us! She is afraid of Black John!"

Slowly Tarzan began to get it, that there was something wrong. It had been a great day for Tarzan. Compressed into hours had been the rudiments of education that with civilized man take years, just as compressed into one sudden swift, moment as he had first glimpsed Mary at the pool had been thrust upon his emotions that cover childhood, youth and manhood. Yet Tarzan was not in a whirl. The very simplicity of life in the jungle was his protection against the complexities of modern man.

For the laws of the jungle are as old and as true as the sky. Man or beast who obey prosper. They who break suffer, are punished and perish. It is the same in the jungle and the hut, the lost village and the cabin, in university and slum, Wall street and the Bowery—the game is the same; only the rules change. Fundamentals are the law of life, inexorable, universal, eternal. Tarzan had much to learn. That was superficial. He had far more to teach. That was deep. The boy and the man were fast friends. Yet there was something supplementary, comple-mentary that each lacked, sought. This wonderful day for each was crowned by it. It was Mary!

So it was that slowly, bit by bit, Bobby succeeded in making his jungle friend realize Mary's peril. And with Tarzan once an idea was realized it was translated into action.

It was dark, now. With his grass rope in one hand, his dagger about his neck, and Bobby caught up in his arms Tarzan issued forth into the night noises and among the prowlers of his jungle.

Once they encountered Numa again. Quick as a flash in the silvery moonbeams Tarzan had loped his rope, swung up into a tree, shot out defiance and again Numa slunk away impotent before his master.

Sometimes from tree to tree, where that showed the mastery of the jungle, again along ground trail or through soft meadow they hurried along. Bobby needed not now to urge on his friend.

They were at the stockade. It was no more of an obstacle than the lines of a tennis court. Tarzan was a three-dimensional human animal. They were over it in a jiffy, Tarzan and Bobby, safe, high up in the crotch of a tree.

Such a sight Tarzan had never seen or dreamed. Excitedly Bobby explained and as he did Tarzan's eyes blazed as he got the idea, more from Black John's actions than from anything the boy could tell. It was more than Tarzan could stand. He had reached the breaking point.

He dropped suddenly, like a panther, before John and Mary. Black John released her, cowering back in utter surprise. Mary recovered herself with a rush, started back.

"It is Tarzan!" The Patriarch and the tribe took it up and echoed it, scattering in wild flight.

An instant later Mary cried out and swept Bobby safe in her arms. Together they watched, clinging.

Black John never took his eyes off Tarzan. Tarzan started slowly toward him. There was no ruse of Black John's that could stay Tarzan now.

They grappled.

From behind trees and cabins now the Patriarch was mustering the frightened natives, arming them.

The fight was swift and short. Tarzan flung the beaten Black John at Mary's feet.

"Oh! Look!"

In terror Mary pointed. The Patriarch and the others were closing in. Tarzan was outnumbered a hundred to one. He turned, saw them coming. But there was no fear in his heart. He drew himself to his full height. Suddenly from his mouth issued the wierdest of sounds— the cry of the jungle.

Tantor heard it and trumpeted. Taug and Teeka heard it and answered. Everywhere, throughout the jungle they heard it—and it was returned.

The Patriarch and the tribe ringed him now. Tarzan faced them. They had no stomach for the fight. But the Patriarch cursed them and gave the signal. En masse they overcame their terror and fell upon Tarzan. Mary and Bobby were swept aside. Tarzan was down fighting overwhelmed by weight of numbers, pinned to the ground.

Meanwhile Black John had revived. He scrambled to his feet, grasping his spear, shouting.

The tribe heard and in an instant they had Tarzan bound to a huge stake in the enclosure, as Bobby and Mary crouched back from the crowd. Black John raised his spear at the defiant Tarzan.

Louder and louder now came the trumpeting of Tantor the elephant. Nearer and nearer he was crashing through the jungle.

Black John smiled at the impotence of it. Tantor would be too late. Defiantly Tarzan called to Tantor. There was a sudden change in Black John's countenance. Tantor was nearer than he had thought—he was at the wall, crashing it!

With a scream Mary turned her head away. Black John had heaved his javelin at Tarzan.

CHAPTER VI
GIANT EMOTIONS

STRAINING at his bonds with his powerful muscles knotted in tense cords Tarzan broke loose from the stake just as Black John hurled his spear.

At the same instant Tantor broke through the stockade and the natives scattered in terror. Black John seized up Bobby and fled after them as Tarzan took the swooning Mary in his arms. The huge elephant lumbered over to Tarzan and knelt. Holding the girl in his arms Tarzan mounted his back. Tantor rose and crashed out of the stockade into the jungle and safety.

Always in times of trouble or perplexity Tarzan was drawn back by a strange power to the lonely hut in the heart of the jungle. Mary opened her eyes, struggled from his arms and stood in this rude shack staring at him.

"Where am I? What happened?" she demanded.

"The witch doctor says he is God." Tarzan in his triumph was child-like. "But he and his people ran from me and Tantor. I am more mighty than Tantor. I am God!"

Mary was aghast. But she smiled, understanding the childmind of the handsome jungle giant. "No, Tarzan—not God—but a man created by God in His own image."

Tarzan echoed the girl's word. "Man." He strode over to the old chest, opened it, and from it he took a picture of a lovely woman. It was Lady Greystroke.

"This—man?" he asked.

Mary took it and shook her head, smiling. "No. A woman."

Tarzan was puzzled. "Woman," he repeated. "She. Like Taug's Teeka?"

Mary smiled and nodded yes. Again he searched the chest and this time drew out a picture of Lord Greystoke in his uniform with the family crest on the photograph. "Man?" he asked.

"Yes, this is a man, like you, Tarzan," answered Mary. "And see, it says Lord Greystoke and there is the crest like that carved on your knife!"

It did not interest Tarzan much now. "Tarzan a man—he?" He thumped his great chest. Mary smiled. "You a woman—she?" Again Mary smiled acquiescence. "You Tarzan's she?"

Mary smiled, bit fearfully, raised herself on tip-toe and impetuously pressed her lips to his face. Tarzan drew back bewildered. He rubbed his lips, a strange smile on his face. "It is like honey that the Sting People hide in the trees!" he cried in the emotions of his first kiss.

Tarzan was like a big child, now. Mary felt her power over him. Yet she feared his physical power over her. Besides, she was tired. She wanted rest. Slowly she made him understand that she wanted to rest alone in the hut. She knew that he would not leave her now, but would stand on guard through the night. Besides there was the bird call if she should need him. Gradually she got the idea into his head to leave her alone in the hut through the night.

Outside Tarzan saw the moon now with new eyes. He swung himself through the trees in sheer joy of living. "Ho!" he roared up at the moon. "King of the night—it is Tarzan, King of the Jungle, defies you! Come down and fight! I will conquer you, give you as a present to Tarzan's she!"

Threshing along in his delirium of love Tarzan made his way through the trees making a wide circle of the hut in the clearing.

All through the night Black John had kept Bobby a prisoner close. He knew that Bobby knew where Tarzan's lair was. But Bobby was defiant.

"No," he stuck to it tearfully, "I won't tell you where Tarzan sleeps."

"You won't!" Black John snatched down a big bull whip from the wall. "This will make you tell!"

Bobby cringed back with terror.

So it was that in the middle of the night Black John gathered four of his boldest spirits. "Tarzan has stolen the woman who would be our queen. Come with me."

Through the jungle the dark five made their way, until on the edge of the clearing they found the hut. Black John could hear Tarzan in the distance bellowing his love-defiance of the moon-god, Goru. It was an opportunity. He posted the four on guard and crossed quickly to the hut.

Mary was just about to retire on an old broken cot, had started to unfasten her scant robe when she was startled by a noise as the door opened with an unseen hand.

"Don't make a sound!" came a thick, hoarse whisper.

She recoiled in terror as Black John crept into the room confronting her menacingly.

"No ape-man shall have the woman I want!" he hissed.

"But I loathe you," she cried bitterly, retreating from him.

Black John grinned in ugly triumph. "I have laid plans to get you out of the jungle when I have located a vast treasure. I know of that will make you richer than the richest woman in the world!"

Mary shook her head. Black John sneered. "You won't?" I hold the winning card—your brother, Bobby. Young woman, be at the village before dawn—or you will never see him alive again!"

"You—monster," gasped Mary.

Nearer could be heard Tarzan's jungle call. Horrified, Mary was weakening at the thought of Bobby.

"If he finds me here with you—" smirked Black John.

"All right. I promise. Now go quickly. Tarzan is coming!"

Black John made a hasty exit, covering up his fear. Mary, filled with dread, turned to the old cot again.

She was apparently asleep when Tarzan entered, covered by an old blanket and a leopard skin she had snatched up from the floor. A moment he stared at her, then reached over and touched her soft shoulder with his big hand gently. Mary, tense on the cot, was pretending to sleep. Inwardly she was full of apprehension. He reached over and picked up the leopard robe she had caught up from the floor. She did not move. Then he vanished through the door to sleep in the open with his covering.

In the morning, full of renewed energy, Tarzan swung himself down to the door of the hut and opened it. His heard stood still. Mary was not on the old cot. He called her name, searched the room, then dashed out of the hut.

Tarzan was indeed a wild man. The honey of that first kiss had turned to bitterness. The beasts and the birds of the jungle went two by two. Must Tarzan walk alone—always along? Tarzan the might was swiftly turned again into the ruthless killer of the jungle. He uttered a bull-ape cry, uprooted a sapling and flung it from him, as he strode along.

In the village they heard the echo of his cry. "Tarzan" the natives cried. "Tarzan is calling to his jungle people again! He comes to kill!"

In Black John's cabin Mary hugged Bobby closely to her breast and smiled. She had heard the call faintly echoing; now she heard the shouts of fear of the villagers, as they scattered. It filled her with joy. Help was coming.

Her joy was short-lived. Through the door of the cabin shouldered Black John in rage. He strode over to a small trap door in the wall. He indicated to her to go through. With Bobby clinging to her Mary obeyed. The trap door slid back behind them and Black John who had quickly followed.

There beside them was a lion pit. In it

snarled a ferocious specimen. Horrified Mary shrieked Tarzan's name. The lion let out a terrific roar.

Just an instant Tarzan hesitated in the village as he heard his name called. It was Mary's voice—and it came from Black John's cabin. His rage changed instantly to worry. Another moment and Tarzan leaped to the door of Black John's hut.

Again the lion roared and Mary screamed. Tarzan entered quickly. Suddenly the door slammed behind him. Black John had thrown a heavy bar. With the other hand he reached for a lever. He pulled it, opening another trap.

Snarling the lion charged through the trap as Tarzan crouched to meet the tawny leap of the infuriated beast.

CHAPTER VII
FLAMING HATE

CROUCHING with his knife ready as the lion emerged blinking from the shadows set to spring, Tarzan quickly straightened himself up to his full height, uttering a peculiar hiss. Still snarling the lion shrank back as though in subjection. He knew and feared Tarzan.

Black John had not been prepared to see the king of beasts slink away from Tarzan. But with a low order of cunning the renegade met the emergency. Under cover he rushed Mary and Bobbie into another of the huts.

Through the village reverbrated the bull-ape roar of Tarzan.

"Tarzan! Tarzan!" screamed Mary, answering. "Tar—"

Black John's grimy hand over her mouth smothered Mary's cry. She broke from the renegade, crouching back. "You thought to trap Tarzan. But even the beasts of the jungle are his best friends—and fear him!" She suddenly recollected, gave the shrill bird call.

Rampaging through the village Tarzan heard. He scattered the natives like so many leaves in the wind. From hut to hut he tore until suddenly he heard the muffled bird-call issuing from one of them. He hurled himself headlong against the thatched wall of the hut. As he crashed through, arms tensed, the fury of battle in his eyes he confronted Black John.

Whatever he might be Black John was no coward. With desperate courage he met the attack of Tarzan. But he was no match for the giant strength of the infuriated jungle king. Tarzan lifted him bodily like a log and flung him to the ground. Before the crumpled villain could even begin to get himself together Tarzan had leaped after him, planted his foot on his neck and drawn his knife prepared to dispatch him as he had hundreds of jungle enemies in winning his kingship.

Mary uttered a cry of horror. "No, Tarzan, No!"

No one but Mary could have stayed his hand. Tarzan desisted and turned away just in time to meet an onslaught of fanatical natives with long spears. He grappled the foremost as Mary flung her body between the attackers and Bobby. Uttering his call Tarzan broke the spear blade from its shaft.

The echo of his call had hardly died before there came an answering roar from the lion.

"Numa!" cried the panic-stricken natives. "He comes to aid his friend, Tarzan!"

The last of the natives had fled and Black John was struggling in his daze to rise when Mary ran to Tarzan. "Quick!" she pleaded, "Before they return."

Tarzan smiled, reached down, swung Bobby to his shoulders then with his free arm about her he hurried the girl into the jungle.

Again Tarzan sought refuge in the lonely hut in the heart of the jungle. This time he had a purpose.

Tarzan did not have to know the word mystery or what it meant. His very actions now intrigued Mary and Bobby as he made them wait on one side of the hut while he dug until he had upturned a stone with which the floor was paved. He reached down, took something out of the hole under the stone, then as he rose he handed a small rusty steel box to Mary.

"Long ago," he explained, "I was found here by Toka of the Ape People. Toka cared for me. And so I grew. One day when I was playing on the floor I dug up this box."

Mary opened the box. From it she took carefully a paper yellow with age. Almost the first thing her eyes fell on was the name, Earl Greystoke.

"Why, Tarzan," exclaimed Mary, "this explains it all—about you—! This is written by Earl Greystoke, your father—"

Puzzled, Tarzan did not understand. He had taken the paper from Mary's hand when he interrupted her with child-like directness, reaching over for the photograph of the general.

"Earl Greystoke—God? Bigger than Tarzan?"

Mary studied both the photograph and the papers he had showed her. "No, Tarzan," she repeated patiently, "Lord Greystoke is not God. But these papers prove you his son and heir."

The jungle man seemed bewildered. "Him—God—bigger than Tarzan?" he reiterated. The idea seemed to worry him.

"No, Tarzan," repeated Mary. "Lord Greystoke was not God. He was your father. These papers prove that you are his son." She tried to simplify the idea as much as she could.

Tarzan was tired of these things that he did not understand. He swept the box and the papers aside impatiently. There was one thing which he did understand and that loomed all-important in his mind just now. "Tarzan a big god—himself— and you—Tarzan's she!"

He started toward Mary. It was elemental love-making. It was ownership, possession. Mary was pleased and started, even frightened as the giant Tarzan came closer. It gave her a thrill to have him feel that way and yet, inst[i]nctively, she moved away from him.

"Oh, look! They've followed us."

Love-making refined or elemental meant nothing to Bobby. He had been at the window. Suddenly his sharp eyes had spied an unnatural motion in the jungle. It was one of the savage villagers crouching, peering through, spear poised at the hut.

No sooner had Tarzan disappeared with

Mary and Bobby than Black John, now recovered, went back to his scheming. He had gathered the returning villagers about him urging them that after all his magic was greater than Tarzan's. He had harangued them until he had them worked up into a high state of passion—in the absence of Tarzan. "Come with me," he shouted. "Save our White Queen!" It had not taken much to lead them out on the warpath again, as he brandished a most deadly looking spear.

Already Black John and his renegades had ambushed the hut. Mary recoiled as she saw them slinking in the jungle. But Tarzan turned swiftly and took her bodily into his arms as he shoved little Bobby back of them for protection. His every instinct urged him to fight for what was his own.

Mary struggled but it was not to get away; it was to restrain him from striding forth to force the combat.

"No, no! Tarzan—they will kill you!"

Even Tarzan noticed that. It was fear for him, not for herself. Bobby had pulled the door shut and a bar on the outside had dropped locking it. Mary was proud of Tarzan's strength and fearlessness but the moment he let her down she flung her own arms around him, holding him. "No, Tarzan! Black John's spearmen are all about us!"

There were still some of the natives who felt the terror of Tarzan in his presence. It was different from defying him when he was absent and they were safe in the village. "Tarzan is more mighty than your magic," faltered one doubter.

Black John sneered. "My magic is more mighty than Tarzan! Surround the hut, before I strike you dead!" Black John was an opportunist. His eye happened to catch gathering clouds on the horizon. "Why, even the storm gods obey my magic!" he shouted.

Mary was having more trouble than ever to restrain Tarzan inflamed with the insolence of Black John in even thinking he might cross the will of Tarzan. "I am Tarzan," he thundered. "No one can take you from me!"

With devilish ingenuity Black John was setting fire to a bunch of dried grass tied to the head of a spear. As it burst into flame he cast it through the air like a wide-flaming meteor until it struck in the thatch of the roof of the cabin scattering far and wide a shower of sparks.

It was only a few moments before the thatch was a flaming mass spreading fast in the rising wind.

Mary snatched up the precious papers Tarzan had showed her and thrust them in her bosom.

The hut was almost entirely in flames as Tarzan, Mary and Bobby ineffectually fought the stifle. Flames and smoke were licking up hungrily behind them as Tarzan burst open the door. The moment he did so a veritable rain of spears slithered at the hapless three. Tarzan took Mary in his arms. There was no going back. Ahead was the tribe now worked into a state of fanatic fury.

CHAPTER VIII
MOCK MARRIAGE

AS a witch doctor Black John had been just a little bit too efficient. That is, he had claimed too much and too soon. The very rain clouds which he had pointed to as obeying his will headed up all too quickly into a veritable cloud burst and in the downpour the fire in the hut was stayed and quenched with a suddenness that was so noticeable to the superstitious natives huddled back from the fury of the storm that they murmered openly among themselves.

"The medicine of the Witch Doctor is powerless against the Rain God. It has failed again!"

Mary was quick to catch the murmuring among the natives. With elation she pointed it out to her hero, Tarzan. Nor was Tarzan loathe to take advantage of the turn of events. He seized up a club, dashed at them and they broke into a retreat that was soon a panic and utter rout as he bellowed his jungle cry at them.

Even Bobby, boy-like, was seized with the lust for battle. He loosened a spear from the wall where it had stuck and slipping past Mary's ineffectual attempt to stop him, charged lustily after the fleeing natives also.

Black John was a cool renegade, crafty, never with his eye off the main chance. Routed though his followers were and inwardly panic-stricken he did not miss seeing that with Tarzan in tempestuous pursuit and Bobby running after him Mary was at least for the moment defenseless.

He doubled on his tracks, crept back of the hut and along the outer wall. Turning back to the hut Mary shrank back in fear and tried to run. It was too late. Black John made a quick leap, caught her by the wrist while with his other hand he covered her mouth to prevent a repetition of her outcry.

Black John was glaring at Mary, the personification of evil triumph, "You're coming back to the village with me and if you make any outcry—" His hand dropped significantly from Mary's mouth to the hilt of his knife.

Mary's hand clutched at her bosom. Black John thought it was fear. But it was the thought of the papers so precious to Tarzan which she had hidden.

"This time," he sneered, "I'll put you where your ape lover will never find you." Black John cast apprehensive glances about in fear of the return of Tarzan, still comporting with his swaggering tone. He caught Mary's arm. "Come along—and look alive!"

Mary's terror of the man mounted when she found that it was neither to the cabin nor his hut in the stockade that he was dragging her. Instead it was to the opening of a passage in the hill that led to a cave. Mary had never explored it, in fact had kept away from it for the reason that she learned that here were the underground ceremonial chambers of the Lost Tribe where high priests held constant vigil. She had heard vague rumors of their sacriligious rites.

Half dragging, half thrusting her Black John penetrated into the shadows of the cave until he came to a wall to which leg and arm chains were fastened. The antechambers had been guarded by two of the high priests, weird, outlandish, grotesque in their native religious robes and headgear, the terrifying effect of which was heightened by the fitful light of torches which penetrated the gloom of the cave only enough to reveal its terrors.

Black John grunted some guttural gibberish to the priests. She knew he was talking about her and she made a desperate attempt to break away from him. With a leer he literally cast her at the feet of the priests.

As he did so the precious papers which she had been clutching in her bosom fell to the floor. Black John saw them and snapped an order to the priests to hold her as he made a sudden move to get them. Futilely she struggled to recover them but Black John merely laughed as he picked them up and ran his eye over them in the murky light. His laugh of contempt turned quickly to one of exultation.

"With these papers, little one, I can return to England and claim the title and the estates of Lord Greystoke." With a leering grin he took a step towards her as the priests held her. "And you—you shall return with me as my wife—Lady Greystoke!"

All at once Mary's fear crystallized into desperate courage. "Never!" she cried defiantly. "I'll die first!"

A malevolent assurance spread over his features. "Either that," he ground out, "or you will die—in the fiery pit!"

Mary continued her defiance in spite of her bewilderment. But Black John merely laughed again in his malevolent assumption of power. "Show her the fiery pit," he ordered the priests contemptuously. "That may change her mind!"

They pulled her along roughly as Black John smiled in malicious triumph and followed into the even darker recesses of the cave. Suddenly one of the priests reached down and threw open a trap. Mary drew back with a scream as long tongues of flame leaped out of the fiery furnace. Black John aware of what to expect was already standing aside, although even the floor was no exactly comfortable place upon which to stand here. The glare of the flames marked his face with an even more sin[i]ster look.

"Which shall it be—marriage with me or—" He did not finish; he did not need to finish. All that was necessary was to point to the fiery pit.

"Not that!" Mary shrank back as far as the iron grasp of the two priests would permit. "Not that!"

"Then your answer is yes?" he demanded.

Mary bowed her head in the glare and heat. Black John interpreted it as assent. He motioned quickly to the priests to close the trap of the pit and take her away.

If Mary had any illusions about her freedom they were quickly dispelled when the priests chained her by each arm and leg to the wall while Black John stood by. "And now," he said, "I shall make arrangements for the ceremony to take place at once."

Their eyes met. Mary's did not waver. "I warn you—Tarzan will kill you!"

Black John's dark face broke into a sneer as his lip curled. "If Tarzan appears in the village, my men will sound the alarm. That," he added impressively, "will be the signal for your death!" He turned his head ominously toward the fiery pit. Then his harsh look softened but it was evil softness, the condescension of wickedness, as he leaned toward her. "You are mine! No one else shall have you! Remember that. Even though Tarzan should escape my men by a miracle, he cannot get here in time to save you! There is only one way in which you can live!"

Mary shrank back against the cold dank wall, helpless. The full horror of the man having all but overwhelmed the delicate, highstrung girl. Without another word Black John turned, motioned to the priests to follow him and they were swallowed up in the gloom of the cave leaving the horror-stricken Mary alone.

In the tunnel that led into the ceremonial cave Black John posted one of the priests on guard near the entrance, then went on with the other, posting him just inside the door. Within the chamber itself Mary was straining at her chains and crying out. She might as well have tried to move the mountain itself or call for help in the middle of the ocean.

Black John strode across the enclosure until he found the chief drummer. "Ah! Sound the wedding tom-toms!" he thundered. Instantly the native dived into his hut and a moment later reappeared with the tom-tom.

At once he began the beating of it. And at

once the village was alive as the news spread.

"Black John is marrying the White Queen!"

Someone else besides the native drummer had heard the order, too. It was Bobby, minus his spear now, and no sooner did he hear it than he set out on a run that gave wings to his young feet. He knew only that this meant danger to Mary.

Scattering the panic-stricken natives before him in precipitate flight Tarzan had gone further than he had intended, through the sheer joy of seeing them run. Thus it was that he had met up with Bobby lunging through the jungle with his spear. Tarzan smiled. "Bobby—brave man-child, bad spirits run before him!" he complimented as he swung the boy on his shoulder and they started back to Mary at the hut.

But Mary was gone. Tarzan called; Bobby called. There was no answer. Bobby was first to voice Tarzan's fears. "Black John has carried her away!"

Tarzan swung Bobby under his arm and crashed through the jungle in the direction of the stockade and the village.

He would have torn his way ruthlessly through the stockade had it not been for Bobby's quick wit. "Tarzan," he cautioned, "not that way! If Black John knew you were here he would harm Mary."

There was a brief argument which ended in Bobby winning his point. Tarzan looped his rope over the stockade, set Bobby down on the inside, then retired outside himself to wait.

Thus it was that Bobby got his first shock when he found Mary was not in the cabin, nor in any of the huts. He got his first clue when he saw Black John issuing from the mouth of the cave. As he followed him, hiding, he overheard the orders to their drummer of the tom-toms. That was enough.

Tarzan's rage swelled as Bobby reported what had happened to Mary and he heard the tom-toms and the gathering of the natives. Quickly Tarzan and Bobby made their plans.

As Bobby appeared before the priest on guard at the cave entrance, tricking his attention, suddenly from behind the powerful hands of Tarzan clenched the guard and strangled him. Again they played the trick with the second priest.

Mary's terror changed suddenly to hope as she strained at her chains. Here was Tarzan.

With his superhuman strength he wrenched one of the chains loose, and started to wrench the other. It did not snap so easily.

From the pinacle of elation John had been suddenly cast to the depth of murderous anger as one of the priests, recovering, staggered to warn him. In a towering rage he seized his long hunting knife, passed another to the priest, and on stealthy, cat-like feet they entered another, secret passage back of the ceremonial chamber followed by the other priest, now also armed with a knife.

"Hurry, Tarzan," urged Bobby. "They will be here!"

Tarzan tore again at the refractory leg-iron.

From a secret panel in the rock wall back of him emerged three shadowy silent figures. Three long, murderous knives were raised in the darkness ready to strike without even a flash of warning.

CHAPTER IX
BLACK JOHN'S REVENGE

SUDDENLY Tarzan sensed the peril behind him. He swung around as the last chain snapped and released Mary, just in time to catch in his grip of steel the arm that was descending with the dagger, in the dark. Single-handed Tarzan was more than a match for his attackers and for the others, also, that Black John had hastily mustered in the emergency.

From a distance the venerable old Patriarch of the Lost Tribe was watching with troubled mein as he saw Tarzan vanquish one after another of the strongest young men of the tribe. His fear changed to a frown as he caught sight of Black John himself slinking off into the jungle. What was to become of them with this new terror loose in the very holy of holies within the stockade? Hitherto they had relied on the craft and cunning of Black John and his so-called "magic." What now?

The Patriarch knew only one law of life. That was to bow to the rulership of the strongest. And had not Tarzan proved himself the strongest of them all? Even now he was giving the terrible jungle cry. A few moments and even the beasts would be there, doing his bidding.

Quickly the Patriarch approached Mary. He bowed low. "Oh, White Princess! Beg Tarzan the Mighty to rule over us—he who is king of the jungle,—lest we perish!"

Mary had always felt a sneaking sympathy for the old man under the tyranny of Black John. She took his arm and led him toward Tarzan.

"Don't strike, Tarzan!" she pleaded as she saw him at once ready to defend himself by attacking even this newcomer. "He wants you to be their Chief—to take the place of Black John!"

At first the mere idea was repugnant to Tarzan. But Mary coaxed. And what Mary wanted was quite a different story. He began to relent, then to be interested, finally to consider as the other members of the tribe gathered about. With aboriginal eagerness they were ready to yield fealty to the new overlord. Tarzan bowed to the honor of the inevitable, and elated the Patriarch turned to address the tribe swearing them to loyalty to the new leader.

There was but one dissenter and he was not in the open. From a hiding place in the tropical tangle Black John listened as he heard himself deposed and Tarzan elevated in his place, listened long enough to realize that it was unsafe for him in that neighborhood, then turned swearing to himself a dark oath to get revenge.

At once the village was in great excitement. It was an event of major importance to have a new chief and it called for a weird and elaborate ceremony of installation. Preparations were at once begun for it and the natives threw themselves into it with a will for it was indeed a great thing to have Tarzan fighting for them, not against them.

Thus it was that when darkness settled down on the village that night the Patriarch and the entire tribe were assembled about the central fire with flares, the priests in weird costumes and the dancers outdoing themselves to make honor to Tarzan.

It was more than even Bobby could stand

after the wild events of the day. He had seen nearly all of the ceremony and his head was nodding so that he was almost asleep. Mary carried him to the cabin and put him on his pallet of straw. It had been a great night for Mary, too. Every honor that was showered on Tarzan was like the gift of a jewel to her. She was tired but she was not going to miss a thing. She covered up Bobby, even thought that in the heat of the night he might need a drink. She took a hollow gourd to fill at the spring outside.

Suddenly a hand, a strangely familiar hand, stole through a hole in the wall of the hut, then another was clapped over Bobby's mouth as he was jerked through the opening of the thatch, and an instant later the devilish Black John slunk back into the shadows of the jungle making his way as fast as he could with his burden.

Across on the other side of the jungle fastness at last Black John stumbled into his secret camp which he had always kept ready against some rebellious outbreak in the tribe. There he had built himself a lean-to and there now he flung the tired Bobby whom he had carried off and then tired out by his forced haste.

Bobby was too sleepy to do otherwise than heed Black John's threat to lie down, for it would have been the easiest thing in the world to have left the boy outside the circle of the firelight a prey to the strange night-prowlers of the jungle.

For a moment Black John listened for sounds of pursuit. Hearing none he also settled down. His quick mind was going over his future course. What should it be? Back again to his life as a beach-comber, searching the sea eagerly for a sign of a ship? He sat bolt upright. Those papers he had seized from Mary! An evil smile overspread his face instantly. He reached into his pcoket and pulled them out, scanning them eagerly in the firelight. Here, then, was his plan, his way to turn defeat into a blazing success. Just let a ship appear and answer his signal and he would be in touch with civilization. That meant that he might use the very proofs of Tarzan's heritage for his own gain. He would be Lord Greystoke, heir to the title and the estates! He fell asleep dreaming of it.

Men of Black John's calibre always fail because they seem never to give their opponents credit for having any sense. They always underestimate them. And anyone that underestimated Bobby was bound to lose out sooner or later.

Bobby had not been lying long before he began to watch furtively between the slits of almost closed eyes. As he saw Black John lose interest in watching him and become absorbed in the papers he had stolen from Mary, Bobby's boyish mind put the situation together well enough to realize that there were compensations for his kidnapping. He restrained himself until Black John was snoring deeply and regularly. And as he did so his own fatigue departed and he felt refreshed with the night air.

At last Bobby decided that the time was ripe to carry out the plan he had evolved. He crept stealthily from the lean-to toward the man asleep by the dying fire with the papers still clutched in his hands. Carefully Bobby loosened them from the almost supine grip now and extracted them. Then as fast as ever he could Bobby backed away from the sleeping villain.

Unfortunately Bobby did not have eyes in the back of his head. He backed right into a bush of brambles, and the long thorns tore his clothes smartly as he repressed his own exclamation of pain and side-stepped. Luck was against him. He toppled over a jar that was in the dark shadow of the bush, smashing it.

Instantly the alert senses of Black John caught the sound. He roused from his sleep, sprang to his feet, rubbing his eyes which adjusted themselves to the darkness like an animal's. His first instinct was about the boy— and sure enough he had fled from the lean-to. He could hear him, too, crashing through the jungle in his frightened haste. It might be death to Bobby in the night. Black John cared nothing for that. If Bobby were dead he would lose his hold on Mary. Bobby was Black John's hostage to fate. He hallowed after the boy and pursued, now trying to frighten him against running into the jungle perils, now seeking to coax him back.

The more he threatened and cajoled the harder Bobby beat it. A little monkey saw him, jabbered and swung along in the trees. But Black John was gaining. Bobby was getting more winded. He stopped to hide behind a bush. That would never do. Suddenly he saw a leopard cub dart into a cave. Black John was coming closer.

Bobby followed into the cave. Outside now he could hear Black John cursing and swearing. "Which way did the brat go?"

It was not many seconds after Mary missed Bobby that she was calling the alarm to Tarzan. Tarzan took it. Here was work for the tribe. He had them all out tracking Black John and Bobby. All night they scoured the jungle fastness and found not a trace. Even Tarzan was without a clue until suddenly, high over head, he heard a chattering. It was one of the monkey people. Tarzan stopped, listened, chattered back, and was off.

Behind him Taug, crafty and cunning, was watching. He had heard the chattering. Suddenly now he, too, descended from the trees directly in front of Mary. HIs powerful arms encircled her and he started to drag her off as he had Teeka.

Black John was just about to enter the cave where he could hear sounds of Bobby playing with the leopard cub when he drew back at a snarl. The mother leopard had leaped to the cave mouth, more deadly than the male as she sensed a possible danger to her cub. Another moment and Bobby was confronted by two gleaming green-yellow eyes and a blood-curdling yowl as the infuriated cat crouched to play with this man-animal, torturing it as in its fiendish nature it did with its other jungle prey before the kill.

CHAPTER X
THE IMPOSTER

TARZAN crouched glaring at the blazing eyes of the panther in the yawning dark mouth of the cave and suddenly getting set by instinct that his life in the jungle had sharpened, leaped. Bobby shrieked as over and over rolled man and beast. Black John from behind a rock stared, his eyes almost popping out of his head. What an opponent was this for him! If he had prayed at all it would have been to his devil-god—and for the panther.

To neither Bobby in the cave nor Black John behind the rock did it seem that Tarzan had a chance. Suddenly Bobby discovered another opening to the cave and dashed out through it—directly into the arms of Black John behind the rock.

"Fork over them papers, kid!" he growled as he seized Bobby roughly and ran his hands over him, frisking him thoroughly.

He found them, ran his eyes hastily over them to see that they were all right, then slunk into the jungle dragging Bobby along by one hand and threatening him if he made an outcry.

"It won't do no good—the panther's finished Tarzan—you don't hear no sound, do you?"

On the other side of the cave on the contrary Tarzan may have looked a bit the worse for wear but was smiling cooly as he slipped his Greystoke hunting knife back in its sheath that hung from his neck. There was one less enemy left in the jungle for him.

He was not so cool as he explored the cave, found Bobby gone, leaving only the cub. He called. But there was no answer from the silences of the jungle, at least from Bobby.

Tarzan turned quicky as a native crashed through in fear to be the bearer of bad news yet more in fear not to tell it.

"Taug has stolen our White Queen!" he panted.

Tarzan was convulsed with fury. He cupped his hands to his mouth even before the native had finished telling what he had seen and let out a tremendous roar that echoed far and wide through the jungle.

Tantor and Numa and all the host that did Tarzan's bidding heard, and answered. Taug heard, but did not answer. Instead he almost grinned his apish triumph as he looked down at the limp form of the fair Mary in his arms powerful enough to crush any heavyweight champion of the world. Mary had swooned and he started off on his half run, half lope with her.

Tarzan threshed his way through the jungle leaving the startled native as he went to gather such a detective strong-arm force as perhaps man had never had before.

Black John heard the battle cry of Tarzan, thought it was for him, redoubled his haste as he fled to the coast with the desperate hope that he might find help.

There is an uncanny luck that seems to hang over evil men of the ilk of Black John at times. It would shake one's faith were it not for the fact that always before it is over such men demonstrate the inate evil in them and in such a way as to point an even more spectacular moral for good than they possible could otherwise.

Black John dragging Bobby along stopped short in amazement as they neared the shore. Not in his wildest dreams had he imagined anything like what greeted his eyes. There was not only a trim steam yacht riding at anchor in the offing, but on the shore was pitched a camp. A careful reconnoitering of it decided Black John on going immediately to it, without parley.

As they approached they saw a rather distinguished looking Englishman in a pith helmet. With him was another man who seemed to be his secretary. Everywhere were blacks busy with tents, the campfire, cooking and other duties. Although Black John did not know it yet this was the brother of Lord Greystoke on an expedition into the heart of the jungle to find any clues that there might be as to the fate of his brother and his wife and baby.

No one could have been more surprised to see white people in the deep of the jungle than was the present Lord Greystoke when Black John walked into his camp with Bobby. They exchanged salutations and it was not long before Black John learned to his utter surprise the purpose of the expedition. As Greystoke explained it Black John's face concealed a crafty smile.

"Why, Uncle!" he exclaimed. "Then I am George Greystoke, your nephew!"

Greystoke was a bit perplexed but Black John followed it up by pulling out the papers he had stolen. Greystoke and his secretary looked them over carefully while Bobby could hardly contain himself at the enormity of Black John's deception.

Finally Greystoke extended his hand. "Then my long search is ended. I am glad to hand over the Greystoke heritage to you."

Bobby could stand it no longer. "He lies!" he burst out. "He stole the papers from Tarzan!" Greystoke and his secretary turned. "Tarzan is your nephew. This man is a cheat."

Black John was equal to the occasion. "Pay no attention to the boy," he waved him aside. "His mind is unbalanced. I've just nursed him through a long siege of jungle fever."

However, Greystoke was no fool; he was not going to accept an identification like this without complete proof. "Of course," he added, "I assume you must have other proofs than these that you are the real Earl of Greystoke. There are certain heirlooms of the Greystokes, for instance, an oddly shaped hunting knife."

"Oh, of course," nodded Black John. "I have the knife in my hut. I have treasured it ever since I was a child. I shall get it." Lord Greystoke nodded. "Please take care of the boy while I am gone. And, remember, he is not himself." Black John hurried away. He was already forming a plan to get the knife from Tarzan.

"That's all a lie, too, about the jungle fever," insisted Bobby as he poured out his story and told of Mary and Tarzan.

"If what you say is true, my boy," Lord Greystoke patted his head, "we shall learn very soon."

They were so engrossed in Bobby that they did not notice that Black John had gone around the tent and watching a moment when the blacks were busy had stolen one from the stack of rifles and disappeared into the jungle again.

Swinging along from tree to tree Tarzan was eagerly searching the jungle for a clue to Mary. At last he caught sight of Taug loping along with the unconscious girl in his arms. Tarzan redoubled his speed and it was not many moments before he had overtaken his arch-enemy. Taug dropped the girl and the two faced each other, knowing that this was to be a battle to the death.

They circled and suddenly Tarzan sprang. They clinched and rolled to the ground, fighting furiously. It seemed as if an unconscious sense of danger called Mary back to consciousness. She opened her eyes just as Tarzan succeeded in getting Taug down and holding him. Slowly he was strangling the brute, just as Mary ran up to him.

"Twice I have saved his life!" muttered Tarzan. "He will no longer trouble you."

He turned from Taug and with a final kick to his helpless body picked up Mary gently in his strong arms to carry her.

Mary was crying softly to herself still about Bobby. It went to Tarzan's heart as such tears go to the heart of every strong man. As he always did when in trouble he bent his steps back to the hut in the jungle. There he laid Mary exhausted on the bunk, turned, and said what seemed the only thing to say. "I shall go search for your little brother." His actions were so rapid that almost before the words were out of his mouth Tarzan was out of the door, looping his rope into a tree and swinging along with a lusty will to find the boy.

Played out though she was Mary managed to pull herself up from the bunk and run to the window. She would have called him back for she had a foreboding of danger, only already he was too far away.

Suddenly, however, she did scream. There in the distance she could make out the form of Black John skulking in the jungle. And he had a rifle! Mary's scream could not warn Tarzan, at that distance.

Tarzan poised himself on another limb for a swing when suddenly Black John raised his stolen rifle, took careful aim, there was a puff of smoke followed by the distant crack of the report and Mary screamed again in vain as Tarzan fell from the tree.

CHAPTER XI
THE STOLEN HERITAGE

TARZAN'S grass rope parted as the rifle bullet of Black John struck it and Tarzan fell like a rock to the ground striking his head on a stone. He lay there motionless as Mary ran as on the wings of the wind and flung herself, sobbing, on him trying to lift his heavy inert body.

At that moment Black John crashed out from the jungle with the rifle ready to finish Tarzan should there be any signs of life left in him. Mary interposed her body between the rifle and Tarzan.

"You can do him no more harm! He is dead and beyond your power now!"

Black John smiled grimly. It was evidently true. Besides, he recollected what he had come for. There was no one in the hut. This was the time to search it without another scene with Mary. She would not leave Tarzan's body now.

He would come back and attend to her later.

Undisturbed now, Black John ransacked the hut. Sure enough, just as he had suspected, there were the Greystoke's heirlooms, the papers left by Tarzan's parents, the books, and, above all, the photographs of his father and mother. Black John was more than satisfied. He crammed the stuff all into his pocket and hurried from the hut back to Mary and the inert body of Tarzan.

"Now that he is dead, young lady," he said brusquely, "you might as well come with me. I shall be the Earl of Greystoke and make you a fine lady." He grinned and was about to seize her.

Mary could hardly control herself for loathing. She had the presence of mind to reach down quickly and draw from its sheath the hunting knife that hung about Tarzan's neck. She held it aloft poised straight at her own breast. "I would rather kill myself," she cried defiantly at Black John, "than throw my lot in with a beast like you!"

Black John was impervious to words like those. He merely smiled his confident smirk. "You'll get over this, my pretty one. I'll be back for you. You'll not escape me. But now I have some important business, important for you, too, the future Lady Greystoke, my wife." He turned quickly and disappeared down a trail.

Bobby in the absence of Black John had been improving the time by pouring into Lord Greystoke's sympathetic ear the story of his friend Tarzan. And Bobby could tell it with boyish enthusiasm that needed no embellishment.

"Lord Greystoke," he insisted earnestly, "this man Black John is a liar and a cheat. Tarzan is your real nephew. Tarzan is a great man. He is wise and he is good. He has the courage of a lion and he is the king of the jungle. All the animals and the natives recognize him as Tarzan the Mighty. Why, once when the people in the lost village laid a trap to catch Tantor, the elephant, Tarzan saved him. Tantor would give his life for Tarzan. So with all the other animals—they love him or they fear him. Why, the natives have even just made him the chief of the Lost Village in place of Black John!"

It seemed that Bobby might have gone on for hours pouring out his story to Lord

Greystoke. Amazing though it was it was evident that this was not the raving of a boy recovering from jungle fever. Lord Greystoke was more than impressed.

"Tarzan," continued Bobby eagerly, "is the only real man in the whole jungle. I know he is your nephew. This Black John who pretends to be your nephew is only a beachcomber. He is no good. Come with me to Tarzan's hut and find him. He will prove to you that he is the real Earl of Greystoke."

"I dare say," agreed Lord Greystoke with more than the usual enthusiasm of an Englishman, "there is a great deal in what you tell me. I shall certainly investigate this Tarzan myself."

The boy was leading the nobleman through the jungle when suddenly they came face to face with Black John seeking them.

"Ah, there you are, uncle," greeted Black John, Judas-like, as he produced the photographs and other papers he had just taken from the hut of Tarzan. "Now you must be convinced that I am your real nephew, the true Earl of Greystoke. These photographs are of my father and mother, your own brother and his wife."

Lord Greystoke took them, scanned them with interest. They were indeed the pictures of his brother and his wife. The mystery was thickening instead of clearing up. He must temporize.

"I have promised this small boy to see Tarzan before I make my decision," he insisted. "He will lead me to the man's hut and I expect to talk with him. After that I can tell you more." Greystoke took a few steps on his way.

To his utter astonishment he found Black John blocking his way with the rifle, threateningly. "This man-beast, Tarzan, is dead, understand?" insisted Black John. "I killed him with this very rifle. And now I am the lost Earl of Greystoke and you've got to believe it!"

"I say!" Greystoke was amazed at the effrontery of the man. Yet he did not dare go too far for he had come on his way with Bobby unarmed and alone and Black John had one of his own rifles.

"Come, up with your hands!" Black John had cast the die and was going to play the game through now. Besides, he smiled at the luck that seemed always to be his. "Back in there!"

He had noticed that directly back of the man and boy was a cave and above the mouth of the cave was poised a rocking boulder left there at some prehistoric geological age.

At the point of the rifle he backed them into the cave and rocked the heavy boulder until it fell over it. There was just a small space left over the top of it, not large enough to get an arm through, much less even the body of a boy. Through this space now Black John hissed his parting shot at them.

"So, my fine lordling! There's nothing to prevent my telling your secretary and the servants when they return from the hunt for you that you have been killed. Then I shall take your yacht and return to merry old England and take my station as Earl of Greystoke."

With a laugh and sneer he hastened along the trail which Bobby and Greystoke had already traversed. He came to Greystoke's tent with all its parapnernalia strewed about. He had decided to make a thorough job of it and at once. Here as he rummaged the tent and the boxes he quickly got out breeches, shirt, pith helmet, everything just as Lord Greystoke had, especially the cartridge belt with an automatic. In a jiffy he was changed from his rags and skins to the snappiest hunter ever outfitted by those in London who know how to do it. He would waste no time in getting away with the yacht and on it.

In her grief and terror as Tarzan lay there motionless Mary gradually began to realize that his body was not cold. She was happily alarmed when she saw a flutter of his eyes, then a tremor of his strong limbs, and finally an effort to raise himself as his eyes opened and he saw her and smiled while she rained kisses on his face.

Little did Mary realize the recuperative powers of Tarzan after the life next to nature that he had led. Tarzan with her aid was himself before she could fairly realize the joy that had come to her after the depth of grief.

Tarzan was ready to go on just where he had left off. She tried to restrain him but he smiled. "Nothing matters," he said in his broken English, "until we find your brother Bobby."

Mary was overwhelmed at this thoughtfulness and again she kissed him. That kiss was like new life in Tarzan's veins. He picked her up in one arm as if she had been some small, soft pet and away they swung through the jungle as Tarzan examined the ground for any signs of a trail.

Nor was it long before he found the footprints of Bobby, and others. On they went faster than Mary had ever believed it possible for a human being to penetrate the jungle fastness.

It was this unexpected sight that greeted Black John as he emerged finally from Lord Greystoke's tent. There in the distance he saw Tarzan whom he believed as dead as a skeleton—and Mary! He was dumfounded and turned back into the tent to grab a gun.

Anxiously now Mary led Tarzan on, for here was a camp of white men, of their own kind. They approached the tent and in it Mary could discern a stranger with his back to them.

"Have you seen anything of a small boy about here, sir?"

Black John tried to disguise his voice as he answered, "No." But there was no disguising that voice to the trained jungle ears of Tarzan. In an instant he had torn the pith helmet off Black John, revealing his evil face to Mary, now thoroughly terrified.

Instantly Black John aimed Lord Greystoke's automatic full at Tarzan's breast. Mary screamed again, but in his fury, knowing nothing of the danger, Tarzan lunged himself full at Black John as that worthy pulled the trigger.

CHAPTER XII
TREACHERY HIGHER UP

MARY shrieked and flung herself forward suddenly to save Tarzan from Black John's bullet. The gun exploded but the distraction was just enough to spoil Black John's aim; the bullet was diverted and harmlessly whipped away wide into the jungle tangle.

"Look out, woman, or I'll get you, too!" swore Black John.

Tarzan watching John seized the opportunity and made a sudden grab for the gun. In a rage Black John struggled with Tarzan to break his hold but in vain. Tarzan wrested the gun from his hand and with the other hurled Black John from him as with both hands he bent the gun into a horseshoe with a sudden twist and flung it away, flashing a scornful look at Black John.

Black John was fearful as he saw this evidence of Tarzan's strength. His eyes flashed about furtively and he grabbed up one of the camp chairs and hurled it at Tarzan. Mary uttered a quick cry of warning. Tarzan ducked and as the chair flew over his head made a dash for Black John. Black John knew he was no match nor was he even a match for Tarzan in ducking and dodging. Tarzan was on him like a flash, caught him, lifted him bodily over his head and was about to hurl him with his terrific strength to the ground when again Mary intervened.

"No, no, Tarzan, you must not! Remember—Thou shalt not kill!"

"Black John try to kill Tarzan." He stuck to it doggedly in the law of the jungle. "Black John must die."

"Please, Tarzan," pleaded Mary, "for my sake—wait,—wait until we find Bobby."

Tarzan relented. He could deny Mary nothing. "What Mary asks Tarzan will give. Tarzan will wait."

Tarzan set Black John back on the ground, then looked about and saw that Mary had picked up a rope. It was her idea to bind Black John so that he could not escape. Black John watched furtively.

"He has the papers, Tarzan, that prove who you are," added Mary.

Tarzan searched him and brought out the papers and trinkets which he handed over to her. Then he completed binding Black John to a stake, and they hastened away to seek Bobby. Black John smiled.

Again Tarzan called upon his jungle detective force, cupping his hands and bellowing his jungle call. And again Tantor and all his host of jungle friends heard and answered.

"Never fear—they will soon find Bobby," he reassured.

Tarzan knew what he was talking about. It was not long before one of the little monkeys who ran chattering through the trees heard issuing from the cave where Lord Greystoke and Bobby had been imprisoned by Black John the muffled cries of the boy as he tried to shout through the slit left open by the huge boulder Black John had rolled over the mouth of the cavern.

Mary was proceeding through the jungle with Tarzan calling little Bobby when suddenly from the treetops scampered the little monkey chattering and gestulating. Tarzan placed him on his shoulder and they struck out again into the jungle in another direction.

No sooner had they approached the cave than the monkey jumped down, ran ahead and perched on the rock that blocked it. Tarzan put his shoulder to the rock and exerted his herculean strength. The rock rolled away and with a cry Mary caught Bobby in her arms.

Greystoke came out blinking into the light as Bobby turned. "This is Lord Greystoke, Tarzan's uncle," he cried.

Greystoke turned from the beautiful girl to the strange handsome jungle man and suddenly uttered an exclamation as his eyes rested on the hunting knife suspended from Tarzan's neck.

"Why, that's the knife I gave, my brother, the Earl of Greystoke."

Tarzan did not take in the excitement of Mary and Greystoke, until Mary as best she could tried to explain it. Then he looked at Greystoke. "You—my people—my flesh—my blood—like Mary and Bobbie?" he asked.

"I—don't know," returned Greystoke

uncertainly. "You certainly look like my brother. You have his knife—and yet—" He paused as he looked over the papers, and Mary told where they had been found and how Black John got them and they got them back. As he put the story together he was convinced. "My search is ended," he said. "We can return to England now and my nephew shall take his rightful position as Lord Greystoke. But first, before I return, I should like to visit the hut where my brother died."

"All right," answered Mary, "we will take you to it."

Meanwhile at Greystoke's camp his secretary and three of the blacks were returning from searching for Lord Greystoke. The secretary came to a sudden stop as he saw Black John tied to the stake. Gun in hand he advanced cautiously.

"What's all this?" he demanded.

Lies came readily to Black John's lips. "A dozen natives attacked us—left me a prisoner here and carried off Lord Greystoke and the boy."

A skeptical smile curled the secretary's lips.

He spoke to the natives and at once they began a search of the camp. "You tell an interesting story, my man," he said, "but I believe the boy told the truth and you are not the real Earl of Greystoke." Black John listened in dismay as the secretary went on, "Lord Greystoke evidently had reason to tie you up—so you will have to remain as you are until he returns."

Black John's scheming mind was working fast as the secretary turned away toward the tent. Suddenly he called to him. The secretary heard, hesitated, then returned.

"Lord Greystoke will never return!" confessed Black John. There was still a sneer of doubt on the lips of the secretary. Black John eyed him and said suggestively, "Now, if I were free, we could return to England—no one would question my right to the Greystoke title and estates—and you would get half!"

The secretary was actually startled by the boldness of the proposition but when he got over the first shock he eyed Black John speculatively. He was considering the idea. Black John hastened to tell what he had done to Lord Greystoke and Bobby and the secretary nodded as he realized that if Greystoke were dead in the panther's cave there was every chance to get away with the scheme.

"Tarzan and the girl have the papers and trinkets," went on Black John, "but there are other things at the hut that will be of use to prove I am Lord Greystoke."

The secretary was at heart a crook and a quick thinker, also. Quickly he pulled a knife and slashed Black John's bonds. Together the two set out, armed and accompanied by half a dozen of the blacks, Black John leading the way to the hut of Tarzan.

Black John had a wholesome respect for Tarzan in his absence. He made sure when they reached the hut that no one was in it or around it and then they entered and began searching for any other heirlooms that Tarzan might have treasured.

"Great heavens!" The secretary with an uneasy conscience had been peering with one bye furtively out of the door as they searched. He had caught just a glimpse of his master, Greystoke, with Tarzan, Bobbie and Mary.

Black John's face was livid with rage. He

turned fiercely, menacing the secretary. "It's too late for you to back out now," he threatened. "You've got to help me! Come on!"

Greystoke and Bobby, Tarzan and Mary stood in the door of the hut. Black John had pulled the secretary around the far side of it and they were hiding. The blacks had also been warned to keep under cover. Greystoke was much affected by his emotions as he pictured to himself the last moments of his brother and Lady Greystoke in this hut. Mary was also touched at his emotions.

"Don't move! Hands up!"

From the dark recesses Black John stepped out quickly with his gun levelled. At the same moment the traitor secretary covered them from the other side. Suddenly from outside the door were thrust a half dozen murderous looking spear heads as the natives came from their ambush at a signal from Black John.

CHAPTER XIII
A THIEF IN THE NIGHT

TARZAN sprang so quickly, like one of his own jungle friends, that he was grappling Black John even before the renegade could draw a bead on him. At the same time from Tarzan's throat sounded again that terrific roar, that unfailing call to the animals of the jungle that always brought them swiftly to his aid.

Tarzan had learned what few tricks of fighting Black John had. But Black John had not even begun to fathom the numberless tricks of Tarzan. Thus it was that Tarzan was almost instantly giving Black John a tremendous beating, while at the same time in the near distance could be heard Tantor trumpeting that he was on his way with help and it seemed as if the jungle had suddenly become alive with beasts.

The secretary saw the beating that Black John, himself no mean fighter, was getting. It was enough for him. He turned and dived through the open window leaving Black John to Tarzan and his fate.

He did not even pause as he passed the blacks with their spears. They were good fighting men and they did not know what they were up against. On sped the secretary. The blacks started into the hut—until suddenly one of them in the rear heard a familiar noise behind him and glanced over his shoulder. There was Tantor coming on now with a mad rush. The black shouted.

There was a peril the natives understood. They turned from the angry elephant and fled precipitately, scattering in every direction, regardless of Black John and the secretary. It was an utter rout that Tarzan had accomplished in scarcely a twinkling of an eye.

In his rage Tarzan picked up Black John and threw him through the very window through which the secretary had dived. He would have preferred breaking every bone in his scurvy body but there was Mary and he had learned that brutality did not appeal to her. He did not even follow him. Perhaps his friends in the jungle would take care of Black John and relieve him of this unpleasant duty.

Instead he merely turned with a smile to Lord Greystoke, Mary and Bobby, apparently unmindful of the heroic manner in which he had saved them from a nasty situation. Greystoke was not so unmindful. His brother had been a pretty good amateur leather-pusher. That was something he could appreciate in his new nephew.

"If I had any doubts as to who you are," exclaimed Greystoke approaching Tarzan in unfeigned admiration, "they are at rest now. You have the stuff in you that will make you worthy of the name you bear."

Greystoke said much more in his enthusiasm. But Tarzan was only puzzled by the thanks that were heaped upon him until Mary took a hand and began to explain partly in signs and partly in simple language.

Tarzan was human enough to be pleased and natural enough to show it. But suddenly he heard a noise outside, smiled, turned quickly and went out. Greystoke and the others followed this strange hero.

It was Tantor who had arrived and was looking for Tarzan. As the latter came from the hut he walked over to the great beast and leaned up against him, thanking him in the jungle gutterals for his promptness, as much as if he had said to the huge elephant, "Thank you, my friend. And if I should need you again, I will call—just as you would call me!" Then he turned and rejoined the others in the hut as Tantor departed.

Greystoke was even more amazed at this by-play between Tarzan and Tantor and immensely impressed by it. What a man this new nephew of his was!

Still, remarkable as it was, this was no life for a civilized Britisher, though it was much to talk about at the club later. Greystoke pulled at his mustache and suggested that they had better be on their way. Tarzan did not understand, but Mary did and she asked time merely to gather up the remaining keepsakes and trinkets of Tarzan, relics of his parents and the past, into bundles which they could carry.

Black John had lost no time in picking himself up after Tarzan hurled him through the window and betaking himself also in the opposite direction from the aroused jungle sounds. He had not gone far when he heard a frightened voice calling for help. He recognized it with contempt. It was the traitor secretary thoroughly scared at being alone in the wilds. Black John moved along as if to leave him to his fate, then paused as another idea flashed over him. He considered a moment then hurried in the direction of the call for help.

The secretary almost fell over Black John in his relief, for a leopard had been lurking near him. Black John lost no time in coming to the point of his plan.

"If Greystoke were out of the way and I had the proofs, couldn't I pose as the son and heir?"

The secretary who had tears of fear in his eyes calmed himself enough to blurt out that he thought he could. Then Black John hurried on to involve him in his plan. "All right. Then you go back to them before they leave the hut. Make them think you're sorry. Tell them you were forced by me to do what you did or I would have killed you, anything. Watch your chance and tonight when they are all asleep, strike

Greystoke, rejoin me and we will put it over and we'll both be rich—and in London!"

In detail Black John hastily sketched his plan, how the secretary was to recover the papers from Lord Greystoke, where they were to meet in the morning, and by dint of threats and coaxing he had the man as pliant as putty.

So it was that just as Tarzan and Mary were leaving the hut with Greystoke and Bobby, the secretary ran up to them breathless and with a flood of words accusing Black John of having almost killed him and then making him aid him under pain of death. It was only when Tarzan had diverted Black Johns attention that he had had a chance to escape from the man and he had done so through the window. It was a plausible story he built up and although Lord Greystoke eyed him sharply he bade him abruptly to come along with them. Black John was watching keenly from an ambush to see how the initial steps In his latest plot worked out. All seemed propitious and he smiled.

The return to Greystokes' camp was uneventful. There was much to talk about and Greystoke was more and more fascinated by his strange nephew the more he saw of him. A fine dinner, the most novel meal Tarzan had ever experienced, was prepared, and they sat far into the night still talking.

Finally it came time to turn in. One of the tents was given to Mary. Greystoke offered to relinquish the other to Tarzan. But Tarzan would have none of it. He had never slept in a trap and he did not propose to start it. The trees were beds good enough for him. So Greystoke took the other tent and the secretary established himself on guard at the campfire and Bobby was wrapped up safely in skins and stowed away with Mary to mother him.

Midnight in the jungle saw the fearful secretary who had been sleepless before the fire began to stir himself. He rose cautiously and looked around. Not a sound from any of them. It was Tarzan of whom he feared most. But Tarzan was asleep in the crotch of a tree. He was doubtful, but he must take the chance. Besides he knew Black John was lurking somewhere in the darkness and if he did not take the chance, Black John would get him before he was safely on the yacht again. He fingered the hilt of his hunting knife.

As noiselessly as he was able the secretary crept into the tent of Greystoke. Hurriedly he bent over him and lightly scratched for the precious papers. There they were—and he slowly extracted them. Greystoke stirred. Down plunged the knife of the secretary as with the other hand he choked back Greystoke's cry of alarm. He felt the man go limp, then stole from the tent and struck out into the shadows of the jungle to the rendezvous Black John had fixed.

His relief was intense when he encountered Black John skulking exactly where it had been prearranged.

"Did you get them?"

"Yes. And I got him!"

"Good! Then let's beat it! What's that?"

Tarzan slept with one ear and one eye open. Even the sound of an unwonted whisper was enough for his trained jungle senses. He had heard something and instinctively he was awake and on guard. It was Tarzan swinging down from the tree and into the camp, to see what was wrong.

The secretary was gone from the fire. That

was wrong. Suddenly he heard a faint noise as if a call for help, muffled. Was it Mary? No, it was from the other tent. It was from his uncle. He sprang to the tent, pushed his way in. There was Greystoke in a pool of blood, calling weakly. Tarzan did not know what to do. He did not need to. Mary had heard and in a moment she sensed the danger, too, and was with them, a gentle and efficient nurse at work at once with the first aid kit of Greystoke.

As Greystoke weakly told what had happened to him from his faithless secretary again the ire of Tarzan was roused. What an introduction was this to civilization. How little do we realize that we humans after thousands of years are not even equal to the law of the jungle. We have retrograded from our golden age into mere efficient, organized, bigoted ignorance born of education. Tarzan sensed it and that something must be done. It was only a matter of seconds before he had raged around and found the trail of the traitor. He was off in the jungle to enforce the lex talions.

"Here, give me them papers," demanded Black John. "I'll keep them until we get out of this." The secretary was loathe. "Here. I say, hand them over. They're safer with me. I'm sure to get out alive!"

There was a murderous gleam in Black John's eyes. He grabbed the secretary and the struggle was short. The secretary was no match for him. He had the papers and was about to fling the secretary from him when he heard a noise that he knew only too well. It was Tarzan on the war path. He turned suddenly. The secretary clung to him, pleading piteously. But he shook him off ruthlessly hurling him at a tree and slipping into the darkness.

The secretary staggered blindly to his feet. A moment Black John stopped. He could hear Tarzan. He could hear the cowardly traitor whimpering. He knew Tarzan would hear and follow that. There was just a chance that he might get to the camp with Greystoke dead, seize Mary, and with all those rifles get Tarzan or at least hold out through the night and make his getaway—with the girl, too!

The secretary stumbled and cried for help as he heard the snarl of a tiger. Tarzan heard it, too. He would have liked to kill the secretary himself. But Mary would never have approved of that. Still, if he kept his hands off and the tiger did it—was not that justice? What more could Mary expect?

The secretary, wild with fear now, leaped and disappeared over a clump of bushes on a bank. An instant later the tiger made the same leap.

Mary was binding up the wounds of Lord Greystoke, giving him water and a little stimulant. He was getting better and stronger under her deft care.

She was intent on her woman's ministration of mercy, bending over him for the hundredth time to ask if she might do anything to make him more comfortable, when she was startled by a noise behind her. She turned and gasped. There in the door of the tent, with only a small boy, Bobbie, and a man wounded sorely even unto death, was she facing the evil countenance of Black John as his villainous hands clutched as if at last he were about to fasten them about his prey!

CHAPTER XIV
MOMENTARY TRIUMPH

"GREYSTOKE you're in my way—and I won't bungle the job like the other fellow did!"

Black John in the entrance of the tent of Lord Greystoke took in the whole situation. The inefficient treacherous secretary had done only half his job. He had secured the papers, but he had bungled the murder of Greystoke. Under the care of Mary his Grace had an excellent chance of being on his feet again, though sorely wounded. Tarzan was not there and by that same token Black John's assurance rose high. He smiled insultingly as he thought how wise he had been to take the papers from the secretary and, after setting him adrift in the jungle, to return to the camp. It was the crowning opportunity and he fingered the knife at his belt thoughtfully.

Mary read what was in his mind and she flung herself between Lord Greystoke and the renegade to protect him. Black John had his eyes fixed on Mary and did not see Bobby slide quietly and unobtrusively out of the tent, then disappear on a run into the jungle.

Black John reached his hand, like a claw, out toward Mary who drew back. Greystoke struggled helplessly to protect the girl.

"Leave him unharmed—and I will go with you!" dared Mary.

Black John laughed with nasty assurance. "You'll go with me anyhow!"

He made a quick move to encircle the girl with his arms, but Mary was quicker. She seized the knife from his belt and at the same time eluded his embrace. As she backed away, but not far from Greystoke, she poised the knife dangerously close to her own breast over her rapid-beating heart.

"Take me—and leave him!" she defied. "Or I will die!"

Black John's eyes narrowed and his voice assumed its trickiest suavity. He agreed to do what she wished but his expression showed that there was some mental reservation. He took a step toward her, but the girl halted him, making him keep his distance. He stopped and at last they came to an agreement. She slowly started ahead after a sad look around at what she was leaving and Black John followed closely, still crafty and menacing. Greystoke tried to rise up and stop the girl but he was too weak.

Along the jungle trail with Black John directing her, Mary proceeded still carrying the knife. Now and then she glanced back over her shoulder at Black John following her but not too closely. His attitude was watchful and ready for whatever opportunity might arise.

Suddenly Mary's foot sank into a hole in the path and her ankle turned with a sharp pain. Before she could regain her balance Black John had leaped. It was just what he was waiting for. He flung his powerful arms about her pinning her arms to her sides and rendering the knife in her hand useless. He almost crushed her in his embrace until she cried with pain and her grasp of the knife relaxed. The moment the knife fell to the ground Black John made a sudden shift, grasping her wrist in his powerful hand and reached with his other hand down for the knife on the ground.

The moment his fingers clasped over the knife, he lifted her up, swung about and carried her struggling back toward the camp. She fought like a young tigress at first but the slender girl was no match for the hardened adventurer. She fought more and more weakly, seemed almost ready to faint from her struggles and her high-pitched emotions. Black John looked down at the weakening girl with eager eyes as he carried her along toward the camp.

Mary was limp and lifeless by the time Black John got his fair burden back to Greystoke's camp.

Fretting and worrying over the safety of the girl and wracked by the pain from his wound Greystoke tried to raise himself up as he heard a noise outside, hoping it was Tarzan. Instead it was Black John with Mary swooning in his arms. Greystoke fell back, closed his eyes. He felt that this was the end.

Black John laid Mary on a pallet of brush in the tent and looked down and over her with eyes full of evil passion. Then he turned and saw Greystoke regarding him furtively. He swung about and strode toward the wounded nobleman, his hand seeking the hilt of his knife.

"I'll finish you first, my lord," gritted Black John with mock deference to royalty. "Then I'll make her mine!"

CHAPTER XV
THE DAY OF RECKONING

TARZAN came up just in time to see the secretary run, and leap over a bank to escape the tiger which was pursuing him, then to see the tiger make the same leap. He swung himself quickly dawn from the tree and hastened toward the spot where he knew the secretary had met his fate.

The body of the secretary was not there. Scattered all about, however were his torn clothes. Tarzan searched through them but he could find nothing of what he was looking for. Gradually he began to realize that his enemy, Black John, had the papers which he was seeking. As he got the thought he raised his head and uttered his jungle cry. Far and wide it echoed. As always Tantor was the first to hear and answer it. But the others heard it and responded, too.

Tarzan did not wait for them to assemble. He cupped his hands and called in the jungle guttural, "Find this man—find this Black John—for Tarzan!"

Even the cat tribe snarled back its answer. At once the whole jungle was on the search.

Suddenly Bobby caught sight of what he, too, was looking for. "Tarzan!" he shouted. "Tarzan!"

Tarzan dropped down quickly beside him. "Tarzan," cried Bobby excitedly, "Black John came into the camp! He has Mary! Come quick to the camp—pick up the trail!"

Aroused beyond measure Tarzan swung the boy up on his shoulder and was off like a flash. The lion and the leopard, the elephant and the tiger, all the denizens of the jungle were scouring the jungle fastness, now, as Tarzan encouraged them. A word from him seemed to redouble their zeal.

Hurry as he might Tarzan could not penetrate the jungle fastness with the speed of the big cats. They had quickly outdistanced him on his mission and as there were many of them they literally covered the jungle.

Black John watching Greystoke was striding with murder in his heart at the defenceless wounded man when suddenly he was arrested by a blood-curdling snarl that sent a shiver down even his hardened spine. He knew that snarl only too well.

Greystoke, prepared to die, looked in amazement as the renegade fell back leaving him unharmed In the face of this greater personal danger to himself.

One look at the lurking danger in those yellow-green eyes and Black John was fleeing panic-stricken from the tent which was but a trap in such a predicament into the open—which was worse.

There was another sound coming from the jungle and it was not of the animals. This was human. Greystoke rose hopefully but weakly on his elbow and called, "Tarzan!" Mary seemed to rouse from her swoon at the sound of the name. She looked around. There, sure enough, was Tarzan—and Bobby! She called, stretched out her arms to him.

A moment and Tarzan had gathered the girl into his protecting embrace, while Bobby tried excitedly to tell her how he had found Tarzan and help

A long low wail as of a gigantic cat seemed to swell out from the jungle—and a wild cry for help of a man. Tarzan did not need to picture to himself the drama that was enacting as Black John fled madly from the infuriated cat, now joined by others of his tribe. With a wild yell and an imprecation on his lips Black John sank down as the largest of the cats leaped. A moment later and the snarling tribe were disputing over what had once been the blackest heart in the darkest of the jungle.

Tarzan merely said, "Black John dead!" It was just one of the commonplaces of his life. Mary covered her eyes and Tarzan picked her up gently carrying her over by Greystoke.

"You are wonderful!" Greystoke exclaimed for once showing quite un-English enthusiasm. "No further proof is needed that you are he whom I sought. Now let us get out as soon as we can. I feel—better."

Mary nodded as Tarzan looked at her inquiringly. Ever resourceful he gave a signal to Tantor who advanced from the jungle now. A moment and Tarzan had disposed the wounded man on the back of the elephant and they were on their way. Greystoke was not at all comfortable as he caught sight now and then of the big cats.

Tarzan merely smiled. "Our friends still guard us," he reassured.

Bobby riding along with Greystoke was enjoying himself immensely. As for Greystoke he was not so sure of it.

So they proceeded until they came in full sight of the lagoon in which Greystoke's yacht rode gracefully and proudly at anchor.

From Tantor's back Greystoke signalled. The signal was answered, and from the yacht at once put out a long boat with a mate and men.

The four watched it as it sped to the shore and finally ran its nose up the white beach. A moment and they advanced to Greystoke, saluting him.

Greystoke was a brick. He turned suddenly, grasped the arm of Tarzan and with a flourish shouted, "The heir of Greystoke!"

Astounded the seamen listened. Unsparing now in his adjectives who Tarzan was, of his poweress and how he had just, again, saved their lives.

Tarzan listened. He might not understand all but he understood enough. Once he looked back at a plaintive call from one of the cats. He walked over toward it, stopped, walked back again.

In that brief moment, Tarzan's quick instinct had set him right.

"I cannot go," he said simply but firmly. "I will stay ... with my friends ... and the tribe that has made me their chief."

Mary was thinking rapidly. Hers was an understanding heart. Greystoke started to protest—then stopped. He had seen enough to realize that it would be useless to argue with this remarkable man. Instead, he watched and listened.

Quickly with a smile Mary raised her face to Tarzan's. "If you stay," she said simply, "I will! We'll send Bobby back with Lord Greystoke, for he is young, but for us—" She paused. There were unwritable volumes in that pause.

Tarzan overwhelmed with joy reached out his arm and drew her closely to him.

"Perhaps," said Greystoke slowly as he

spoke to Tarzan, "you have chosen wisely. Who can tell? But first come to the yacht. There the captain can make the girl yours, really yours."

Tarzan heard, but doubtfully. It was plainly written on his face that he thought Mary was his already. But he hesitated as he saw her face until Mary nodded to him that it was all right.

As the sun sank that night Tarzan stood with Mary upon the lookout hill one arm about her while with the other he waved at the Greystoke yacht bearing Greystoke and Bobby back to civilization. Smaller and smaller the boat faded in the gloaming until finally Tarzan turned and the other arm also encircled Mary. In both their hearts they knew they had exchanged civilization for happiness in the sight of the God of nature.

(The end)

www.ingramcontent.com/pod-product-compliance
Lightning Source LLC
Chambersburg PA
CBHW020628250626
47154CB00004B/1714